WHY THIS IS AN EASY READER

- This story has been carefully written to keep the young reader's interest high.

- It is told in a simple, open style, with a strong rhythm that adds enjoyment both to reading aloud and silent reading.

- There is a very high percentage of words repeated. It is this repetition which helps the child to read independently. Seeing words again and again, he "practices" the vocabulary he knows, and learns with ease the words that are new.

- Only 172 different words have been used, with plurals and root words counted once.

  Almost one-half of all the words in this story have been used at least three times.

  Almost one-fourth of all the words in this story have been used at least six times.

  Some words have been used 11, 15 and 18 times.

ABOUT THIS STORY

Raccoons are intelligent and playful by nature and their antics delight young children, in life and in books. Here the author tells, as an easy-to-read story, of an actual experience his family had with a raccoon.

Children will enjoy learning more about the habits of this lively animal, and of other woodland creatures. Through such study even young children can be helped to grasp the basic ecological idea that animals are essential to human life.

Robber Raccoon

Story by THOMAS LAWRENCE
Pictures by RICHARD CUFFARI
Editorial Consultant: LILIAN MOORE

WONDER BOOKS · NEW YORK
A Division of Grosset & Dunlap, Inc.
A National General Company

Introduction

These books are meant to help the young reader discover what a delightful experience reading can be. The stories are such fun that they urge the child to try his new reading skills. They are so easy to read that they will encourage and strengthen him as a reader.

The adult will notice that the sentences aren't too long, the words aren't too hard, and the skillful repetition is like a helping hand. What the child will feel is: "This is a good story—and I can read it myself!"

For some children, the best way to meet these stories may be to hear them read aloud at first. Others, who are better prepared to read on their own, may need a little help in the beginning—help that is best given freely. Youngsters who have more experience in reading alone—whether in first or second or third grade—will have the immediate joy of reading "all by myself."

These books have been planned to help all young readers grow—in their pleasure in books and in their power to read them.

Lilian Moore
Specialist in Reading
Formerly of Division of Instructional Research,
New York City Board of Education

Library of Congress Catalog Card Number: 73-156275

ISBN: 0-448-05958-4 (Wonder Trade Edition)
ISBN: 0-448-03488-3 (Library Edition)

There was a big old house
by the woods.
For a long time
no one lived there.

Then one day a family came

to live in the house.

The mother and father were

Mr. and Mrs. Newman.

The boy in the family was Ben.

The girl was Alice.

They all liked the big old house

by the woods.

But they had lived in the city.

And the old house seemed very quiet.

"My, it IS quiet here!"

said Mrs. Newman.

"It's so quiet, it's spooky!"

said Ben.

One night the Newman family
was watching TV.
"What's that?" said Alice.
"What's what?" asked Ben.

"That noise," said Alice.

"I hear something funny!"

"It's the TV," said Ben.

"No," said Alice.

"I hear something outside."

"I don't hear anything,"
said Mr. Newman.
"I don't hear anything,"
said Mrs. Newman.
"And it's bedtime now."

Ben and Alice went to bed.

But soon Ben cried, "What's that?"

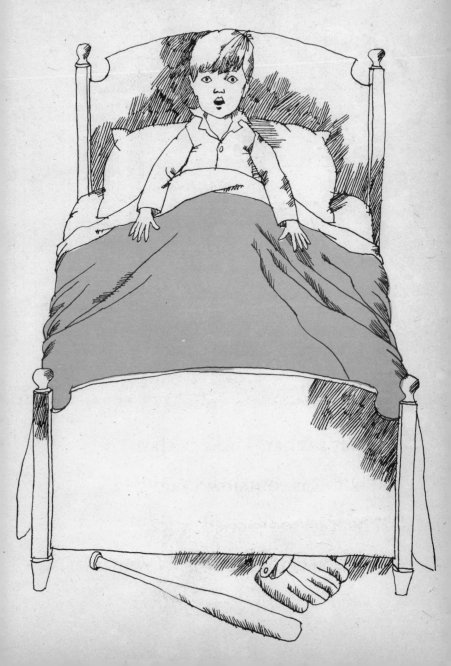

"What's what?" asked Alice.

"That noise outside!" said Ben.

"I hear it, too!" cried Alice.

"Go to sleep," said Mrs. Newman.

18

But then there was a bang.

BANG! CRASH! BANG!

It came from the back of the house.

Mr. Newman put the lights on,

and they all ran out

to see what it was.

No one was there.

"I told you it was spooky here!"

said Ben.

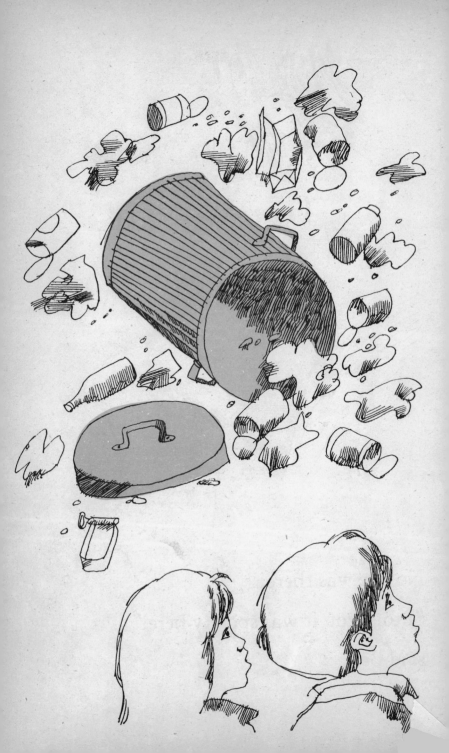

Then they saw the garbage can.

It lay on its side.

And the garbage was all over the yard!

"Oh!" cried Mrs. Newman.

"Someone pushed over

the garbage can!"

"Maybe it WAS a spook!" said Ben.

"I'm scared!" said Alice.

They put the garbage
back in the can,
and went back to bed.

The next night the Newman family

was watching TV again.

"What's that?" said Ben.

"I hear it, too!" said Alice.

"It's coming from the window.

I'm scared!"

"Something is watching us!"

cried Ben.

"I can see it at the window!"

"I see it, too!" said Mrs. Newman.

"It looks like a robber!" cried Alice.

"Oho!" said Mr. Newman.

"It's a robber, all right—

a garbage robber!

It's a raccoon.

HE pushed over the garbage can!"

"A raccoon!" cried Alice,

and she laughed.

The raccoon was sitting

on the window, looking in.

"Look at him!" cried Ben.

"Say, he's watching TV!"

Mr. Newman went to the door.

He was very quiet.

Then he opened the door
and cried, "SHOO! SHOO!"
The raccoon jumped down
from the window,
and ran into the woods.

"There!" said Mr. Newman.

"I scared him away.

He won't come back!"

"He was funny," said Alice.

The next morning the garbage

was all over the yard again.

And the next night,

there was the raccoon,

sitting on the window again,

watching TV.

"Look!" cried Alice.

"Robber is back!"

"Hello, Robber!" said Ben.

"You like TV, don't you?"

"He IS funny!" said Alice.

Mr. Newman went to the door.

He was very, very quiet.

He opened the door

and took the water hose.

WOOSH! SWOOSH! WOOSH!

The water was all over the raccoon.

He jumped down from the window
and ran into the woods.

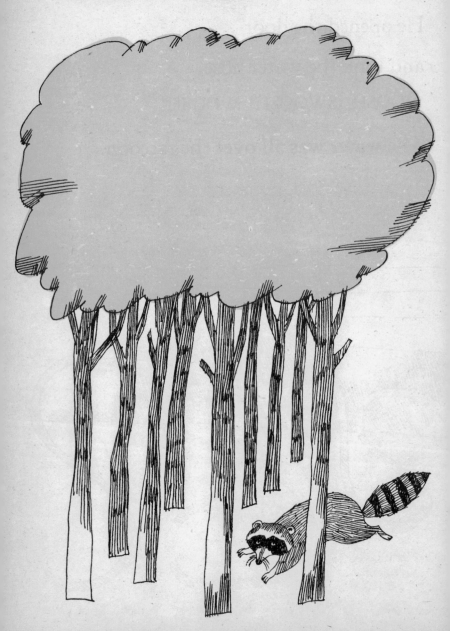

"There!" said Mr. Newman.

"That garbage-robber

won't come back!"

"Poor Robber!" said Alice.

"He looked so scared."

But the raccoon did come back.

The next morning the garbage

was all over the yard again.

That night, too,

he came looking for food.

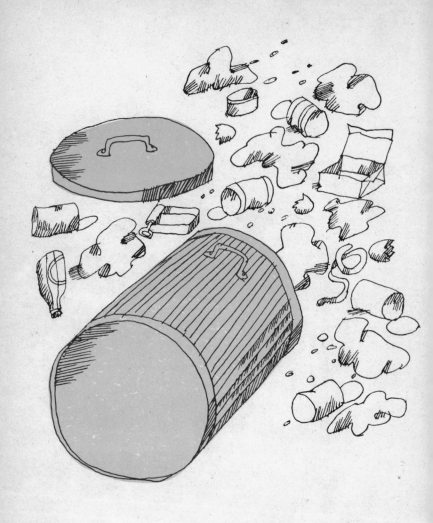

Again he pushed over the garbage can.

Again the garbage
was all over the yard.

"Look at this yard!"

cried Mrs. Newman.

"Can't we stop him?"

"Yes," said Mr. Newman.

"I am going to stop him!"

That night he put the garbage can

in the tool house.

And he hooked the door.

"Poor Robber!" Alice said to Ben.

"Nothing to eat tonight!"

But that night there was a big
BANG! CRASH! BANG!

"It's Robber!" cried Ben.

"He got into the tool house!"

They all ran out to the tool house.

"Look!" said Mr. Newman.

"See the way he got in!"

Mr. Newman hooked the door again.

"He can't get out," he said.

"And I am going to stop him for good!"

"No! No!" cried Alice.

"Let him go!"

"Let him go?" said Mr. Newman.

"Then he'll come back

for the garbage again!"

"Let's put some food out
for him at night," said Ben.
"Then he won't push over
the garbage can."

Mrs. Newman laughed.

"Yes. He can have a TV dinner!"

"All right," said Mr. Newman.

"We'll see."

He opened the door.

And the raccoon ran back

to the woods.

The next night

they put some food out for Robber.

"Put it on the window," said Ben.

"Then he won't be scared

to sit there again."

That night the raccoon did not go

to the garbage can.

He came to the window.

He saw the food and ate it all.

He sat watching TV, too.

"Let's put the TV over here,
so he can see better," said Alice.
The raccoon looked very happy.

After that, he came every night

for his TV dinner.

And they all watched TV together—

Mr. and Mrs. Newman,

and Ben,

and Alice,

and Robber.

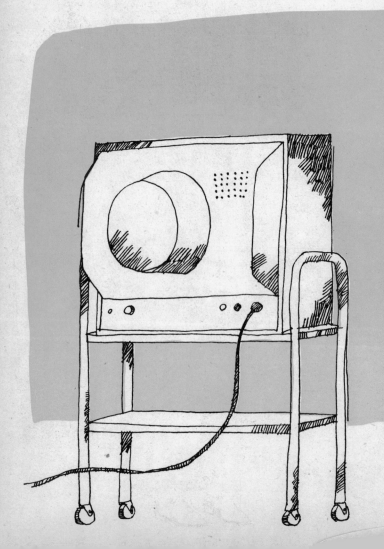